THE PENGUIN POETS

MEETINGS WITH TIME

Carl Dennis lives in Buffalo, where he teaches literature and
creative writing at the State University of New York. A recipient
of a Guggenheim Fellowship and a grant from the National
Foundation of the Arts, he has published five other books of
poetry, most recently *The Outskirts of Troy*.

MEETINGS

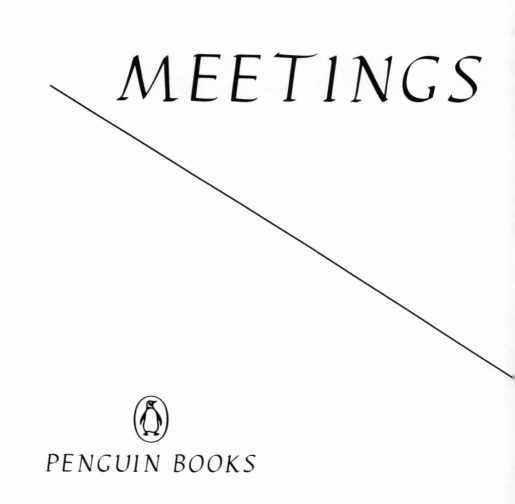

PENGUIN BOOKS

WITH TIME

CARL DENNIS

PENGUIN BOOKS
Published by the Penguin Group
Viking Penguin, a division of Penguin Books USA Inc.,
375 Hudson Street, New York, New York 10014, U.S.A.
Penguin Books Ltd, 27 Wrights Lane,
London W8 5TZ, England
Penguin Books Australia Ltd, Ringwood,
Victoria, Australia
Penguin Books Canada Ltd, 10 Alcorn Avenue, Suite 300,
Toronto, Ontario, Canada M4V 3B2
Penguin Books (N.Z.) Ltd, 182-190 Wairau Road,
Auckland 10, New Zealand

Penguin Books Ltd, Registered Offices:
Harmondsworth, Middlesex, England

First published in the United States of America by Viking Penguin,
a division of Penguin Books USA Inc., 1992
Published in Penguin Books 1992

1 3 5 7 9 10 8 6 4 2

Page 75 constitutes an extension of this copyright page.

LIBRARY OF CONGRESS CATALOGING-IN-PUBLICATION DATA
Dennis, Carl, 1939–
Meetings with time/Carl Dennis.
p.   cm.
ISBN 0 14 058.683 0
I. Title.
PS3554. E535M444   1992
811'.54—dc20   91-5059

Printed in the United States of America
Set in Garamond No. 3

FOR MY BROTHERS

Aaron Dennis and Robert Dennis

CONTENTS

MEETINGS WITH TIME

THE PHOTOGRAPH

The background's blurred, so I can't be certain
If this showboat is docked on a river or a lake,
But the clothes of the dancers on deck
Make clear it's summer in the early forties,
And the long shadows suggest it's almost sundown.

No way to guess the song the couples are dancing to
But it looks like most are enjoying it.
The sadness that seems ingrained in the late light
Is the usual sadness of photographs, not theirs,
The feeling that comes from wondering
How few of the dancers welcome the light now.

And if I see them as ignorant, too confident in the future,
It's only because they're dancing in my childhood.
No reason to believe that the chubby man in the foreground
With his hand on the waist of the smiling blonde
Hasn't stepped back often to observe how his life
Is almost half gone and then returned
To press the moment more eagerly than before.

Here he is, back with the blonde girl,
Whose smile seems nervous now, who may be wondering,
When he's silent, if he's drifting off.
Did she say something she shouldn't have,
Or is he distracted by the man with the camera
Focusing by the taffrail?
Is he troubled to think of himself as old
Looking back on a photograph of this moment
When his heart was younger and more beautiful?

•

Don't worry about it, I want to tell them.
Don't waste your time with recollection or prophecy.
Step forward while the light and shadows are still clear,
The sun, low on the water, still steady.
Enter the moment you seem to be living in.

DEFINING TIME

If it's like a river, the current is too much for us,
Sweeping us past a moment we're still not used to
Out to the void of the not-yet-come.
Should we resist, wherever we are,
Or be reconciled?
It seems to bring us gifts. Each day
Arrives as a fresh basket of bread.
Our right hand no longer can touch our left
Around the girth of our Buddha bellies.
How can that be if the minutes of the day are fish
Nibbling away at us till our bones show through,
Nibbling away at our friends, our houses?
Let's try to ignore it, whatever it is,
As we do the thin air of the Himalayas
When we climb, breathless, to pray for enlightenment.
Can we really ignore its earthy mass
As it lies between us and the thing we hope for?
A long wait till the train goes by
And we can cross the tracks into the evening,
Our favorite time. At last we're walking after dinner
On our ritual mile to the great magnolia.
There it is, glimmering at the end of the field.
Just a handful of whatever time is
And we'll be standing beneath its branches
Looking back at the poplars we're passing now.
How young we were back there, we'll say,
How confused and moody in that early era.
We need more time to consider it,
More than the dole allowed us at any moment,
The nickels and dimes.
We need to unfold time on the table like a map,

With the years gone and the years to come
Colored as vividly as the moment,
Proving how little it means to say
Time has gone by, passed through us
Or around us, and left us old.

WE AND THEY

How rushed they were, those who believed the soul immortal,
With no time for a second opinion about doctrine,
No time for a trial period,
If death that very night might splinter their door
And carry them off to endless bliss or torment.
How different our unhurried, thoughtful pace
As we make comparisons, sipping our tea
On this snowy evening close to the fire,
Breathing the sweet tang of burning cherry.

Did they please their god enough, they had to wonder.
We have to wonder only if we've pleased ourselves,
If we rode the trolley to the last stop
As we promised ourselves to do
Just to see what the country was like
Beyond the practical traffic and grooved streets.

They had to remember what they'd been told.
We have to remember simply what we found
At the first turn of the meadow path.
Was it really a beekeeper with his hives?
Was it really three women
Dressed in the black and white of nuns
Herding cows in a yellow pasture,
Soft shouts and cowbells?

If they forgot the truth, it would cost them dearly.
If we forget, we can still bring it along unawares
Stuck like a burr to our hat brims,
A seed that may open later
And scent the air without our knowing.

Whoever breathes it may feel lucky,
Even those we wronged.

And if those we wronged won't finally forgive us,
Should we let it weigh us down
As it weighed on the people who believed the soul immortal?
All we need is the strength to forgive ourselves.
Pointless then to complain our strength too small
To turn the calendar back to the page before
For a few corrections.

MY GUARDIANS

Not aloof like the famous sky gods,
They keep just one lesson ahead of me,
As uncertain as I am about final things,
Stumped yesterday in Bible class
By the verses that now stump me.
They can't resolve the question
About heaven's kingdom,
How far it lies if it lies within.
They're only an hour or so in front
As they walk home after the concert,
Asking themselves what I'll be asking soon,
Where exactly the music's gone,
Whether the difference between what is and was
Is as vast as it seems and as final.
I'm walking their narrow trail across the country.
The embers of their fire are still warm
As I make my fire and snuggle in,
Happy, as I fall asleep, with the thought
That I'm keeping my true pace,
Not so slow that I lose them,
Not so quick that I pass them unawares.
When I'm lost, I know I've arrived
At the same spot where they were lost,
My wavering steps in the thicket
Proof of my loyalty, my tentative circles
Tramping their circles deep and clear.

ONE DAY

One day I'll make it up to them,
The people I didn't do well by. I'll buy a boat.
I'll throw a boat party just for them.
Plenty of food and drink and music
For those who lost out when I wasn't in the mood
To teach or listen, to inspire or be inspired.
Not in the mood to climb beyond mere taste
As my measure of the world
And invite the woman in the garish straw hat
Reading now on the dock across the inlet.

And I'll invite the clerk in the bookstore
Who knows the guidebook I need for Italy
When I visit near departure day,
The serious one who reads about cathedrals
In her free hours, who could use my ticket
To greater advantage.
Now her glance makes me feel guilty,
But then I'll make it up to her,
Steering my boat for an hour
In any cove she chooses.

Guilt doesn't produce cathedrals.
The architect of Chartres didn't feel guilty
During his work day, though after hours
He may have knelt on modest church floors,
Remembering parents he didn't honor enough
Or friends who needed more time than he budgeted,
Who are also to be invited on the boat ride.

Now I'm not ready to worry about them.
But then I'll do what I can to make my boat
Seem like a prize they might have dreamed of.
And when one of them glimpses a spot on the water
And calls to the others, "Look there!"
I'll look the hardest.
And if I see nothing, I'll try to picture it
And hope it will make the moment
Live long in their memories
Whether or not it lives in mine.

TUESDAY AT FIRST PRESBYTERIAN

Though he wheezes a little, and is stooped, and fat,
Our speaker this evening at First Presbyterian
Warms to his subject in the chilly church hall,
Not afraid to expose the greed of the big polluters
Or the sloth of the small. A man with a mission,
Who's willing to take the planet under his wing
As he might an orphan, who deserves a poem in a high style
That can lift a lowly subject like recycling,
The use of trash as raw material.
The odds against his success are longer by far
Than the odds in many stretches of hexameter.
Whatever Odysseus does to charm a king and queen
Famous for courtesy as they linger over wine,
Reclining on couches in the marble banquet hall,
Is nothing compared to reaching us few in the pews
As we sit here fretting over colds, delinquent bills,
Problem children we have to run back to.
Ten minutes of facing us is enough
To make our speaker drift to an island
Farther than a sea nymph's hideaway.
We can see him walking the beach collecting driftwood.
We can see him resting in the hut of a forester.
A note on the table points to jars of nuts and raisins
Cooling in the dark under the floorboards.
A map marks the secret path to the brook.
Just imagine the blessed few he wants to find there,
Kneeling by the clear pool, cupping their hands.
But now he's rowing back to our church
To resume his lecture on mortal rivers
Flowing through fragile drainage basins.

For his sake we should pay attention,
If we can't be moved directly by the water itself,
Slaking the thirst of us all, the just and unjust,
In smoky city streets and dusty farmlands.

LOCAL GOVERNMENT

If on the long trip to Libertyville
Reason gets to drive, having got up first,
Heart insists on its right to detours.
An hour in the village we used to live in,
A stop at the old house, an exchange of stories
Under the lilacs, beside the rusty flagpole.

It's the day for separating the powers
Hoarded before by a single sovereign,
The day we have to stop for the senses.
Cramped by the car, they insist on tramping the woods.
The rest of us follow behind in single file:
Heart regretting it didn't come here more often
In its younger days, when it had more stamina;
Reason on the lookout for snakes and bears.

And then it's time for lunch and a nap.
Vigilance is the price of liberty
But trust is required as well
For each of us to lie back in the grass
With both eyes closed till everyone's rested
And we're ready to drive on again.

Just before sundown, we sight the spires of Libertyville
And pause a moment at the polling place
So each can vote for the project of his choice:
Courthouse repair or a bigger band shell
Or a longer pier at the lake for the fishermen.

And then, from many doorways, we walk down Main Street
To the fire hall festooned for the dance.

A lively band, but no one has to take the floor
If he doesn't want to. No one has to watch.
There's always good talk around the refreshment table
On the state of our union, the predictable factions
Making the predictable discord,
And the unpredictable music still to come.

THE WINDOW IN SPRING

These weed-grown car hulks rusting in my neighbor's yard
Could be read as tokens of disdain for my neatness
Or as mere indifference to my feelings
If he weren't civil in other ways,
If he didn't take in my papers
When I go on vacation and forget to cancel.

When the eyesore rankles, I tell myself
He could be cooling his flesh with gloomy reminders
Like a hermit contemplating a skull
After the fall of Rome, killing off his hunger
For any abiding place on earth.

On my side of the fence, my garden
Already green, my apple trees and Japanese plums
Proclaim the triumph of husbandry
Dear to the yeomen of the republic,
Disciples of Jefferson.

I was the confident boy in grade school
Shouting the Pledge of Allegiance,
A natural patriot.
He may have been the nervous boy in back
Mouthing the words he couldn't feel,
Destined from the first to be a stranger.

Could be there's a cold mother behind him
Or an absent father, whose father in turn
Lost all he had in the Great Crash.

.

It's a free country when two perspectives like ours
Live side by side without rancor.
No one strolling our block can complain of boredom
Or a lack of options. Door-to-door salesmen
Won't prosper here unless they can vary their pitch,
Masters of many strategies, not merely one.

They tend to choose my house,
The house of a man who clearly cares about upkeep,
Gutters and siding, while my neighbor's junkyard
Seems, in its want of pretension,
Attractive to Witnesses for Jehovah,
Who come Sundays in pairs,
Bibles in hand, to fish for souls.

One of them could have been the girl in my grade school
Whose parents thought the Pledge a form of idolatry,
Who sat, hands folded tight, in silence.
If my parents had raised her, she'd be at home now
Weeding her flower garden or watching the news.

But here she is, or someone like her,
Venturing up my walk as the Bible commands.
She's going to ask what truth I rely on
To save the world, and what's my plan exactly
For convincing my neighbor he isn't stranded in Sodom
With no escape car while the streets are burning.

HAVEN

It can't be Athens, this town
We don't inhabit but carry with us,
For here Socrates hasn't been tried and silenced.
Here he's still at his post on the curb,
Challenging any citizen who pretends
To be an expert on the good life.
And the young still gather to watch
As the proud man is discomfited.
But here, instead of vowing revenge,
As he might in Athens, the man feels grateful,
Eager to get home and report that fame
And power aren't as interesting as confusion.
"What a day!" he mutters to himself,
Pausing at the grocery
For a gift of pomegranates and plums.
We can't see his face as he waits in line
In this town we've never lived in,
But we know he's happy, just as happy
As the brother of the grocery man
Who lives over the store in one bare room,
A saint who just this moment
Has shown his passions the door
But not with the rancor common in other regions,
Not with the hate.
He wishes them well, a good home elsewhere.
And now, in the sudden quiet, he sits on his bed
And leafs through the town bible for inspiration.
Why not the chapter where Ahab forgives the whale
Or the one where Lear decides not to divide
His kingdom after all but to dine with Cordelia
In the main hall, off the best plates?

16

"What should we do," he asks, "with your sad sisters?"
Before she can answer, the saint jumps from his bed
And offers to walk the girls to the waterfront
And teach them how to hear the waves.
The sea that in other towns
Labors under a curse of silence
Seems here to have made a vow
Simply to let the land speak first.
The waves lap at the dock while the moon
Glides over streets we've never sauntered,
The haven we needn't see to praise.

ADVENTURE

When we're tired of adventure, there's always Chekhov,
The challenge of a story like "A Journey by Cart,"
Where nothing happens that hasn't happened
Hundreds of times to the heroine,
A schoolteacher for thirty years.
She's made the monthly trip to the city in the provinces
And collected her salary, twenty rubles,
And now she's on her way back.
Twenty pages without incident
On a long day's bumpy journey by horse cart
To the ramshackle school, in the meager village,
Over a muddy road she knows too well.
Nothing happens to show her she's wrong
For wishing she could have lived instead in Moscow,
City of her childhood, and never become a teacher.
Need forced her, not faith in the calling.
And what faith could have lasted anyway
Out here, where schools are forgotten?

Are we supposed to notice something she's missing?
Is this a story where the heroine,
Preoccupied with her losses,
Fails to detect the delights available?
It's spring, after all. The snow is almost melted.
The woods smell piny and the air is clear.
Can spring be a substitute for a friend,
For someone who listens?
The landowner splashing by on his horse,
Handsome and smiling, slows down to chat,
But he isn't going to propose to her.
Their lives are too different, she sees,

And she's too old. He seems to like things
Just as they are, unmended.
He could have paved the swampy road
If he'd wanted to.

The cart bumps along again and nobody's different.
Even if we send her a hundred handbooks on charm
And she memorizes each one,
She'll remain where she is, in the cart with the driver,
Stubborn Semyon, who refuses to keep to the road,
Despite her urgings, in his quest for short cuts.
And again the cart bogs down and fills with water.
Again the sugar and flour she's bought are ruined,
Her socks soaked and her feet numbed
By the time the roofs of the village edge into view.

"Don't plod on like this. Start over again
In a city with real choices," we'd call from our chairs
If we thought our voices could reach so far.
Now as she waits in the cart for a train to pass,
We want to believe she's resigned and hardened.
Too bad she glimpses in a flashing window a face
With her mother's high forehead and glossy hair.
That's all it takes for Moscow to flood back,
The easy talk in the bright parlor,
The piano and the goldfish bowl,
The girl she was, still young and gaily dressed,
Awakened from a dream of thirty years.

And then the vision's gone and the train.
And here's the village. The story's over.

Do we leave her there?
Do we let her go in alone
To light the stove in her frosty bedroom,
Our sister, who's growing old with us,
Whose crossroads are all behind her?
We have to get back to Moscow,
To our family, to our friends who miss us.

From the window of the train we glimpse her
Huddled in the cart back at the crossing.
Any words of advice we think of shouting
She's thought of long ago on her own.
Just time enough for a nod and a wave.
Then we sit back with the wish
She could read the story we've read
And see her life carried over into art,
Generous art where she's the heroine.

THE BILL OF RIGHTS

You're free to imagine many lives
Though only one's allowed your body,
The body you didn't choose,
Small-boned and thin like Grampa Wheelock's.
Among the songs your elders sang
You were free to pick the one you preferred
And sing it with your own inflections
To the baby sister you were asked to watch.
It was your decision to save half your summer pay
For the teachers college your uncle went to,
To see its closeness as an advantage.
You were free to walk home on the route you fancied
From Ferguson Elementary to the woman you chose,
The sweetheart with your sister's long hair
And the dark eyes of Miss Gorse,
Your Latin teacher in high school,
Who told you you'd go far
If you learned to trust your feelings.
Nobody forced you to buy a house
Near the sycamore trees you climbed as a boy.
Its features pleased you most
Just as you're pleased this sunny Sunday
To climb the ladder and clean the roof drains,
Scooping out mud and sycamore leaves.
And now you choose to pause in your work
And look out over the valley town.
There's the Dalys' slate roof
And the Hendersons' shingles.
There's the smokestack of the bottle plant
And the blue patch of the water tower.
This must be one of the vistas held out to you

Before you were born, one of the many
You were free to choose from.
And now you're free to guess what spirit
Guided your pointing hand that day.
You're free to wonder who whispered in your ear
As clearly as your daughters are calling now,
"Come down, Dad. Come down."
They want to show you the flowers they found
Streaked like the ones you picked for them last fall
Behind the school you sent them to.

THE ANTHROPIC
COSMOLOGICAL PRINCIPLE

Maybe the new theory is true, and the odds
For intelligent life beyond our planet
Are as slim as they were here,
And the only voices ever to reach us
From beyond will be our children's,
Our earth in a thousand years the mother of colonies
On planets never before inhabited.

Long after the sun swells in its final flare
To consume our world, they'll remember us
Just as immigrants here remember the old country in stories.
The Earth will sound to them like a garden,
More a land of myth than of history,
Its green valleys and blue skies incredible,
The way its grasses climbed the hills untended,
The way its birds alighted in groves nobody planted
To trill phrases nobody taught them.

A house like this one, on a street like mine,
Will be a house from a dim, heroic age
When their own fate was decided. Just as I stay up late
To study a narrative of the Civil War
And marvel how close the country came to dissolving,
The great experiment cancelled, the slaves still slaves,
So they will marvel as they study our hostilities
How close we came to spoiling their chances,
Their galactic cities bombed into fictions, their farms,
Schools, churches, opera houses, and union halls
Sponged from the blackboard with the crowds
Cheering on the dock on Regatta Day.

•

Are they real or not? That's the question
That has them worried. Are they waiting on a road
Reachable from the starting point of today?
Impossible to imagine how remote I'd feel
After rummaging in a trunk all afternoon,
Searching for proof that I paid my taxes,
If I found a letter proving I was never born,
That the mother who might have been mine
Ran off on her wedding day and was never heard from,
That I'm only my would-be father's fantasy
As he lies in his empty house on his deathbed
Dreaming of the life he might have lived.

Today I seem to be real as I stop for groceries.
I may be moody returning to the empty house
I promised myself to fill, but not so lonely
If I think of the distant, stellar observers.
What voices deeper than reason and will
I've failed to hear isn't so hard a question
As why I've been fated to decide their destiny.
And what's my strategy for the day, they wonder,
To prompt them to practice songs of joy,
Not dirges?

THE MIRROR

This mirror returning the light it's given
Doesn't reflect enough of me to be trusted.
It settles for the face of a man who's dying.
It says that the blue in the tie he's wearing
Is far grayer in tone than the blue cap he wore
Years back on his first trip to the playground
When he first noticed the sky.

Not a hint in this mirror
Of the self that remains unaltered,
That wades in the rill of time for refreshment
And then climbs out to shower and dress
And dine in the cool of evening on the patio.

Even in the matter of surfaces
The man in the mirror adjusting his tie
Can't manage to be convincing.
The way he favors his right hand
Suggests he's retrained himself to fit in,
To be a member of the majority.
Too late he discovers everyone else
Who's chosen the mirror has changed too,
And he's back where he was, only clumsier,
Stuck in a room where the books read backwards.

This evening he's going to stay home and brood
While I go off to the gallery.
I want to remind myself how much can be done
With two dimensions and a little genius,
How the world of three can be made immortal.
The trees in the paintings

Root down below the frame.
They rise above it to the hidden canopy
Where families and tribes bestir themselves,
Flying in from the wind to rest,
Then flying off in great migrations.

This mirror, jealous and lonely,
Will be waiting up when I return,
Anxious to show me a face that proves
I'm still the person I was,
Just older by an evening.
Don't pretend you're any happier,
It keeps repeating;
Don't try to convince yourself you're growing wise.

UNFINISHED SYMPHONY

Not far from here, as we stroll to the square at sundown,
An old man, writing in his room,
Resists the wind-borne noises of traffic and street games,
The click of heels in the cobbled alley.
He's nearing the end of his great project.
He's almost ready to prove that couples like us
Are strolling to the only square available
In the only world we could be strolling in.
However chosen the moment seems to us,
From where he sits it's always waited
Patiently in the half-light for us to arrive
Over the only road we could have come.
And even when we turned down side roads
To explore the villages, we were still approaching,
Even while unfolding a blanket in the meadow
Beside a stream, sharing a taste of the local wine,
Napping beside the willows.
That's what his love for the truth
Seems to be pushing him to prove once and for all
Though now a breeze from the world of might-have-been
Reaches his window, and he smells the grass himself
And pauses a moment in his argument.
The hardest part's to come, the part where he shows
How the continent had to be settled as it was,
How the Indians had to be waiting for the Conquistadors,
How their ancestors, eons before,
Had to wander across from Asia on the land bridge,
Dancing their Tartar dances, singing their songs.
Down the coast they ventured and inland,
Wrapped in blankets their dark-haired women wove,
Dark hair in long braids that swayed

As they walked in silence behind the dray.
Outside the window, a car door slams.
The old man steadies himself to go on
And show how necessary it was for them to vanish
With their deerskin dresses, their brooches of bone.
He'll finish soon if he doesn't imagine them
Pausing on their trek a few yards from his house
To camp for the night. No going on without them
If the women start combing their hair out
Or sing to the sun their songs of sundown
As they always do.

WAKING ON SUNDAY

These chimes blowing in faintly
Don't want me to abandon my bed
And get a grip on the morning.
They want to be heard before they're as lost
As the table where my mother sat me down
To say how important it was to plan ahead
And think of the good I could do
If I didn't live for the moment, one day at a time,
And didn't forget my family's good examples.

Time to lie still and listen, not to get up
And continue my study of vanished nations,
Their rites of marriage, birth, and burial,
The growing tension between nobles and commoners,
The few who worried about justice
And the many who refused as the bright tapestry
Of the state unraveled.

Last Sunday, when I dragged myself across town
To sit in the half-dark of the nursing home,
My mother recognized everyone in the album
But pushed it away, pained to compare
The woman she is now with the woman she was
When the chimney of the missing house
Poked through the leafy canopy.
This Sunday I'm going to lie here quietly
And savor the dawn concerto.

Peace will come without me if it's meant to come.
New inventions may turn the trade balance around,
A smaller transistor, an engine that runs on air.

So what if the country isn't first anymore?
Other countries deserve their chance in the sun.
Rome fell too, after all,
And England lost her empire.
History moves in cycles and doubtless one day
We'll be lifted to the top again
Though it's likely I won't be around for the ride.

Driving back from the nursing home,
I paused by the lake and tried
To concentrate on the gulls and sails.
It seemed they always wanted to be there,
Out on the water, pleasing themselves,
Losing themselves in their graceful pastimes.

Where they went that evening
Is where this day will go
With the work I've set aside for the morning,
The afternoon stroll,
The supper with a friend or two on the patio.
A day that won't be welcomed elsewhere with chimes.

Not chimes like these, so bright and piercing,
Whose first notes ask me to lie here listening
And keep them in mind as the last begin.

THE WINDOW

Outside the few rooms of embodied life
The field of the never-to-be embodied
Stretches in all directions.
Step to the picture window and look.
That's you going to college in Paris or Prague.
That's the wife and children you'll never have
As they load the car for the trip to the ocean.
Their spaniel, Princess, already dozes in back
Among the stuffed donkeys and dolphins
That Gretchen and Sam will need to sleep with.
Fifteen minutes a day to consider these phantoms
Isn't too much to ask.
The pain you feel looking at what you've missed
Proves that escape isn't your motive.
Why you live as you do and not otherwise
Is hard to say, but at least you know now
It's not from failing to imagine other lives.
And aren't these moments at the window
Part of your life too, a part you've chosen?
Inside the house, the calendar tells the seasons.
Outside, it's the season you wish, spring or winter.
It's a boulevard or a country road, mountain or harbor.
Inside, meadows in Cambodia smoke and groan.
Outside, they're never invaded.
The monks are climbing the grassy hill
To ring the golden temple bell.
It peals out over the roofs of Asia,
Over the caravans trekking through the Urals.
Inside, Vienna floats on without its Jews.
Outside, the Jews have grown old and died
Just like the Gentiles, one by one.

Their children hurry by,
Late for piano lessons and auctions,
For jury duty and dinners
In natty checkered suits and black robes,
Short skirts and long, conversing in accents
You have to imagine for fifteen minutes a day
If you want to free yourself once and for all
From the idol-worship of history.
Main Street will fill with the swagger of the actual
But you won't bow down anymore
As you unload the car, back from the ocean.
The sun will pass in parade, its trumpets and drums
Proclaiming this day chosen from all the others,
But you won't be taken in again.

FIGHTS IN KANSAS

Hours after the students of the Tri-Counties
Have wandered home in the early November dark,
The lights at Madison Middle School are still burning.
In the quiet classrooms, in the company of a globe,
The teachers lean at their desks, the best ones,
Wincing and muttering over their midterms.
Wind bangs at the window of Mrs. Kulick's room
As she figures how to redo her schedule.
No hope now of reaching the shores of the Renaissance
By Christmas vacation. The class is stuck with the Goths
As they pillage the flourishing cities of Gaul
In the month that should have witnessed the Dark Ages
Gradually brightening, the revival of commerce,
The church growing more learned and liberal.
She can hear the armies of light and dark
Clanging their shields all over Kansas,
And the news from the front isn't hopeful.
More of her students refuse to ponder the dead
Because the dead can't ponder them.
Is it pride that makes them embrace their ignorance
Or fear of change? Why should the thought of change
Be as painful for them as it was for Cain,
Who knew his failures but tried to hide them?
That's what she wants to know as the wind
Careens across the Tri-Counties, howling.
And why don't her methods of arousing shame
And interest, that worked before, work now?
Has the slow expansion of freedom
From the few to the many, the plot of history,
Bogged down for good at the edge of Kansas?
She needs a free year to ponder the problem,

33

A year off from her voice,
Which has grown shrill, she knows, and scolding.
A shame she can't afford it.
What about teaching another subject at least,
One freer from the weight of time and chance?
Algebra, say, where the mind works purely,
At play with problems of its own devising.
Even then, she knows, given the mood she's in,
She's likely to insist on its harsher lessons,
How a small mistake at the start will lead,
By the irresistible laws of factoring,
To a massive discrepancy at the end.
Go back, students, she can hear herself repeating.
You won't pass till you get it right.
You won't get it right till you pay attention.

THE INVALID

Today they'd have found a way to get me and my chair
Up the thirty steps of the high school, but then
It seemed impossible, as if the ramp had yet to be invented,
As if two strong boys couldn't carry a skinny girl.
Hearts weren't smaller back then; my friends were loyal.
They visited me at home just as you do now.
But imagination was more confined.
Even my parents couldn't think of a way around it.
And I too learned to see it as a fate
I was foolish to complain against.
Of course I managed to learn at home
More than my friends learned at school,
Scored higher on achievement tests,
Grew more curious about the world.
Still it seemed I was waving from the dock
While they sailed away to the future.
Now I know that metaphor was mistaken.
I too have lived a life, though given the choice
To live it again as it was or with one amendment
I'd choose to live it without the polio.
Wisdom isn't the only thing worth having.
Wiser or not, I'd have felt more free.
Free or not, I'd be richer now in memories,
No small matter for an old woman like me
Sitting in a sunny yard under a plum tree,
A blanket on my wasted legs in mid-July.
Not that I don't take comfort from what I've done,
The way I resisted anger and envy
And worked to make my fretful disposition serene,
The wishes that lead to disappointment abandoned,
Worked to live in the moment like this plum tree.

Whatever it's planned to do it's doing now
Between the garage that needs to be torn down
And the fence that needs repairing.
I've tried to be like a character in a play
Who is nothing but what she says and does
With nothing held in to fester between scenes
While the crowd goes out to the lobby for a smoke.
What about dinner, they ask, at Roma's or André's?
What about starting over in Fresno or Spokane
Where people are rumored to be more sensitive
To genius of the subtler kind?
I hope it isn't merely ignorance of its death
That makes this tree look tranquil,
Or its saintly diet of air and water,
Which has always been too pure for me.

THANKSGIVING

Praising the farmer who took me in
The night my car died in the snow
May be too easy a way to test my skill
In praising what should be praised.
His good cheer may have been mere temperament,
His patience merely the outgrowth of his parents' patience.
So maybe I'll praise his parents too,
The gift of their best years to his playroom.

And if he didn't choose his principles,
I can praise his principles for choosing him,
The first to elbow their way through the crowd
Milling outside his nursery,
How they pushed him to love the movie at the Tivoli
Where the hero walks off the boat from Europe
With a dog, eleven dollars,
And a ticket to his uncle in the grain belt,
Where ten years later, mayor of Altoona,
He won't abandon the helpless to racketeers.

And if his will is too weak to manage his feelings,
I can praise his feelings for pulling him on
As gently as the horse he rode as a child
Jogged him beyond the barn and orchard
And back again before nightfall,
Before a storm blew in like the one
That stalled my car, stranding me among strangers.

That snowy night, awakened by a call from the road,
The farmer gropes for a light
And pulls his boots on without debating.

If he has no choice, if he can't remember his options,
I can praise forgetfulness, the blessing of habit
That prods him to follow his father's example,
Hard at first to manage without muttering,
Hard once for his father too.

ON MY FIFTIETH
BIRTHDAY

Now I'm as old as my father was
When less than a year was left him.
His good deeds couldn't lengthen his life by a day.
What's left of them now, after thirty years,
But ghostly images?

Last night in my birthday dream,
Coming home to a house sunk in the ground
Past the first floor windows,
I found him sitting alone
In the unlit foyer, his head in his hands.

Something he'd left undone still worried him
When he should have been looking down
On the past from a restful star
Where the just dwell, looking down
On an earth grown small and make-believe.

Instead, he was stuck in a dark foyer
Grieving, it seemed to me, though we didn't speak,
That he'd left me his doubtful habits,
Not the ones he trusted,
That he'd failed to put the pain of his youth
Behind him before he married.

He must have assumed that the book of his life
Was closed when his life closed.
Now, because of me, it lay open,
Open to amendment, and not the last page only
But the early ones as well, the rebuffs
His mother received as a girl,

The dreary summers his father spent as a boy
At the stodgy resort where he had no companions.

Whole chapters of his life have been blown away
And lost, not carved on the stone walls
Of a tomb chapel to shame the death gods.
And still his case isn't closed.
The evidence is still being gathered.
What happens now finds room in the margins
That seemed before too crowded for addenda.

MILDEW

Till now a subject mentioned only as a metaphor
To stand for mustiness in the soul.
But here we have the genuine article
Growing on the north wall of my neighbor's house
That's cost him too much already in upkeep.
Black streaks over blue paint that was guaranteed
Against fungus of all kinds, returning each fall
After its spring treatment of bleach.
He scrubbed the bottom story himself
And would have done the rest if he weren't spooked
About ladders since last year, when the gutter
He tried to unclog pulled loose.
Black streaks and a musty smell in the guest room
That stumps the experts. Long before now
He guessed he was only a transient on the planet.
Now it's clear his house is a transient too
Though this evening its lights are burning warmly.
In a minute his Thanksgiving guests will arrive
Having outdone themselves with their walnut stuffing,
Having added new stories to their portfolios.
Their cheerful, spirited talk will fill the kitchen.
He won't interrupt to ask if they can explain
Why his is the only house on the block
With a mildew problem. Bad luck, maybe,
Though in an earlier era it would be a warning
To turn from a world he's loved too much.
But what other world steps forward now
To offer its services? And even if it did,
What deserves more of his gratitude
Than his clapboard guardian against wind and rain,
A basement haven for Ping-Pong on winter evenings,

41

An attic skylight for reattaching to stars
The names washed off by the daily drizzle?
Mildew creeps to the house unseen and suddenly
Scales the walls. But not for him anymore
The temptation of the underground passage
Past the enemy line to a hidden harbor
Where he can still imagine a rowboat waiting.

NIGHT WALK

At midnight, when you hit a snag in your essay
Describing the light only a few can love,
The few who are most awake, do what I do.
Stroll on Main Street past the lighted store fronts.
Pause to peer in the window of Spiegel's Appliances
Past the dishwashers and floor fans.

You should recognize the watchman slumped in his chair.
It's our butcher, yours and mine,
Moonlighting here as he's done for years
Ever since Brenda asked him for a sailboat
Like the one in the cigarette ad,
Complete with cabin, deck chair, and flag.

After you've pitied him for a while, as I have,
The way he's mortgaged himself to tinsel,
Boats and beauties, while the time grows late
And the first page in the book of life
Is still not filled, notice how peaceful his sleep seems,
The sleep of a man happy to drowse through weekdays
So he can snap awake on the weekend
To Brenda dangling her long legs from the bow
Or lying back in her chair, eyes closed.
Why climb the lookout if he has all he's ever wanted?
Why not crawl back and forth on his knees,
Scrubbing the deck down while she dozes,
Or polish the chrome, already rusting?

And after you've asked yourself, as I have, if her smile
Can really last him all week in the undergloom
Of meats and motors, assuming she's smiling at him,

Not merely at the wind for stroking her face,
Ask when the truth you've followed has once smiled back,
Once dropped a note on your plate praising your loyalty.
"Brenda," his tombstone will say,
If the carver wants to record the love of his life.
And what about yours? What word
Would you like lovers and loners to read
As they stroll on Sundays the shady, municipal graveyard,
What truth you loved in your few moments of clarity?

IN THE WAITING ROOM

The nun on the bench in the depot, consulting her schedule,
Is bringing a sackload of gifts to her sister's children
Just west of Plattsburg and bringing her soul
To the hour of judgment it's destined for.
She's here and not here
Like the small man with his headset tuned so loud
She can hear his tape of Spanish work songs.
He's floating south to the country he can't return to.
That's why the fat man at the video war game
Looks to him like a colonel bombing a union hall.
That's why the people dozing on the benches
Look like citizens who want to sleep late
And ignore a noisy minority in the street.
Now he shakes off the comparisons and pins his hopes
On the job in the Plattsburg diner his cousin owns.
With the player off, he can hear the two boys
On the bench behind him arguing over the All-Star Game.
They're halfway back from their father's house in Albany
To their mother's in Plattsburg, and still
They can't agree on the starting lineup.
When the nun looks up at them, they simmer down.
Their love of merit and justice, she surmises,
Could make them superior priests one day
If they can leave the Greek passion for glory behind
For a grown-up faith in mission.
Tomorrow the *Beacon* will print the lineup,
But even today's paper is full of interest
For the gray-haired black man with a lunch box.
Every word holds him, as if he believes that here
The secret of his life might be revealed
Somewhere among the marriage licenses,

Birth and death announcements, pictures of summer hats.
It seems that ribbons are back in style,
Which should please his wife, with her flair for color.
Strange after all these years in the East
She wants to settle where it's always spring.
The weather of Plattsburg is too similar
To the weather of the coal town where she was raised,
An ignorant little girl who guessed somehow
That the only place she'd ever laid eyes on
Wasn't near the outskirts of her real home.

EVOLUTION

Now the statistics are in, we can see
How unconvincing our story is,
Packed with too many hairbreadth escapes,
Too many changes in climate at the final moment.
Dust clouds from a passing shower of meteors
Deadly to plants required by our competition
But not by us. Nothing here for a reader
Who expects a plot to be probable.

The reef pushes up and blocks the inlet,
And the new-made lake silts into marsh,
Choking the fish that adapted over eons
To life in open water, to storms and sharks.
But the freakish lungfish, slow and clumsy,
Cakes itself in mud and dozes through the dry spell.
The flood that sweeps the lowlands
Drowns the burrowers, sober and industrious,
While the one drunk, snuggled in a hollow log
And snoring, is lifted up.
He bobs along on his one-man ark.
He bumps awake next morning on a mountain,
Yawns, rubs his eyes, and gapes.
Our father, who vows never to drink again near bedtime.
So much for proof the fit win out.

This photo of Dad and his boys
Wading in Shadrack Creek Sunday before last
To fish for salmon can be no more real
Than the fairy tale about salmon
Wasting their strength flailing up the rapids.
Might as well credit the fitness of sister eel

Crawling without hands and knees from wells to rivers,
Swimming without a map to the far Sargasso
To join the mating dance of mermaids and mermen
If the sea happens to be calm enough.

No power that claims to be practical
Would choose to embody itself like this in history.
And yet with a little effort we can work up something
To prove how likely it all is,
How suited we are to the sandy soil we spring from,
To clay or loam, marshy or dry.

OEDIPUS THE KING

Hard to forgive Freud, the exposer of fictions,
When he borrows the name of a great mythical king
To cover our common wish not to share mom
With anyone, not even with dad.

Oedipus, solver of riddles too hard for us,
Freud's inspiration and mentor,
Teacher and pupil of one mind with the Sphinx
That man is the mystery,
Three people at least in one.
But even Freud, with all his interpreting,
Didn't manage like Oedipus to save a city.
Vienna could have done without him,
He knew, and would go on as before,
Winning and wasting.

We never imagine Oedipus one of us
Except for a moment, just after the plague arrives,
When he vows to rid the city of its pollution,
To root the murderer out, no matter where.
We too could have made a mistake like that.
But when the question changes slowly
To who his parents are,
We would have stopped, as the prophet advises,
While the king, suspecting the worst, presses on.

Freud may have taken the facts, however painful,
As evidence that we're only human,
Alive and desiring.
But Oedipus chooses to be guilty,
To blind and banish himself

And go the gods one better, the father gods
Who didn't love him as a father should.

As for his mother, if he has one then,
It's the earth, who feels him tapping
Her breast with his cane
As he hobbles along outside the walls.
"Where are you going, dear Son?" she calls.
"For you the door to my dark house stands open.
No other house will take you in."

INFIDEL

If I chew these sesame seeds slowly,
As the book advises, and do my rhythmic breathing,
I may end the year comparing myself to Buddha,
Thinking of myself as his companion.

No more wasting my energy on my will,
The will afraid if it ever stopped wanting
I'd disappear. Head forward,
Shoulders stooped under its sack of ambitions,
It butts its way through the crowd.
It halts in clearings to count its losses.

Now I can turn to meditation and vision
If I chew these sesame seeds slowly,
Walking behind myself at a saving distance,
Glancing around at a world not seen before.

Soon I'll be free to play, to leave my projects behind
And wonder what it's like to be a stone,
Or a tree, or the dog asleep by the lawn chair,
Or the woman in the chair, gray-haired and frail,
Knitting a sweater for her daughter's baby.

To be them, and then to leave them.
To hope they're not as stranded in what they are
As the blue flowers in the yard at the corner
Which seem to keep shouting only one name,
Blue flower, blue flower.

Just a mouthful of sesame seeds and salt
To neutralize the acidity of the blood

And maybe in a week or two the fretful yin child
Will be a contemplative, joyful yang.

And if I can change, my friends can follow
If they're willing to be more flexible
And don't insist, as they have till now,
On their own vivid, unchastened perspectives.

Strange to love those who resist me,
Who block the sidewalk when I go exploring
And won't give ground, who force me
To step aside with my ears ringing,
My eyes watering, and move on

Under awnings that flap their colors
As awnings do, under lindens
Shaking their leaves as lindens will
When they want to refresh themselves
In gusts from the mountains, gusts from the sea.

THE MESSIAH

Now the Messiah's come
And we wake at last confident of our talents,
Free of the flesh that merely wants to sleep late
And star in a dream of adoration,
The schoolteacher who loves both of her suitors more purely
Still has to choose between them.

And even though both, grown suddenly selfless,
Are willing to yield if it makes her happier,
The one not chosen feels bereft
And returns to his paintings with a darker palette
Though all the windows in his loft face south.

Now the Messiah's come, he's ready to do a roofscape
With the reverence befitting tar paper and shingles,
Stovepipes and chimneys. Still it will take a decade
For his execution to match his vision,
A decade he doesn't have.

When his father calls feebly up the stairs
To ask about supper, the painter,
Now the Messiah's come, doesn't begrudge the recess.
It's no longer a case of joy and duty in contention
But of two joys on a day not long enough.

Were it longer, he'd have knocked off early
And joined the protest at city hall.
Now the Messiah's come,
The mayor isn't underpaying his gardeners out of greed
But to save more taxes for charity.
Does mercy come before justice or justice before mercy?

The issue seems pretty clear to the painter
As he stands by the sink, peeling onions.

And clear to his friends like you and me
As we talk, after the protest, at the coffee shop.
It seems a shame, now the Messiah's come,
That our talk is still less permanent than the rain
Falling now on our country to succor seedpods.
Does this moment water something inside us
That will blossom later, or is growth only a metaphor
To sweeten the sour thought of change?

It's growing dark on the street.
The waitress stops at our table to light the candle.
It should never burn down
If this is the kingdom of the Messiah.
And our friend the painter, if he comes tomorrow
Hoping to find us, should be proven right
In his stubborn faith that we're still waiting.

MY MOSES

Time to praise the other Moses, the one who concludes
That the bush isn't really burning, as he first supposed,
Just backlit in red by the setting sun,
Magnified by the need of a runaway to be pardoned,
To pull his shoes off and receive a vision.
The Moses who, when he lifts his staff,
Can't part the waters, who has to wade in
At low tide and hope for the best.
Nobody drowns. Nobody's following. The twelve tribes,
Sluggish after a hard day in the quarries,
Didn't find his lecture on the virtues inspiring.
And Pharoah was willing to see him go.
Good riddance, what with his praise of creation
That gouged the work month with holidays.
Now he's wringing his clothes out on the other side,
Relieved it hasn't taken him any longer to realize
He isn't much of a prophet, that he hasn't the gift.
Free now of the journey to the Promised Land
And the wars with the natives, he can settle down at once
Whenever he pleases, and be happy even here
In the country that disappointed Columbus,
That wasn't the hoped-for shortcut to spices.
Happy even on this block of mine, my neighbor,
A civics teacher at the high school,
Who leaves the gate to his yard unlocked
So the neighborhood children can pick the berries
Before the frost comes and leaf smoke rises
From small, mute fires he's lit himself.

MORE SNOW

Snow overnight, and the meekest man on the block
Rejoices at dawn to see his neighbors humbled,
Demoted to the ranks of shovelers, just as he is,
Their big cars buried in drifts.

And the man whose virtues have never been recognized
Notices sadly how the Philistines to the north,
Who've let their trash for years blow in his yard,
Whose deafening pickup bangs his fence,
Look just as responsible while they clear their drive
As the saint to the south who's late
For errands of mercy to shut-ins.

So late he doesn't have time this morning
To chat with the widow next door,
Who's already shoveled her steps twice
And now is using a broom on the snow crumbs.
Old as she is, she still isn't sure
What drives her to be the tidiest on the block,
Whether she's still trying to please the father
Who didn't praise her enough
Or to please herself, or set a good example.

Whatever the prompting, someone, she reasons,
Has to counter the drift of her neighbors
Toward skimpy paths, one shovel wide,
And challenge the sloth
That leads to the poor life of hideaways.

Someone must make the effort
To change mere repetition

To ritual in the church of snow
Whose doors are rumored to stand open now,

Beckoning all of us into the street
Before the plow comes
For the snow dance and the simple snow songs
Whose words we don't believe we know.

REMNANTS

Alpaca blankets, resin, hemp, and coffee
Are still unloaded and loaded at docks
Just as they were eighty years ago
When my mother, newly arrived from Russia,
Holding tight to her mother's skirt,
Stepped ashore, wide-eyed, into the New World.
And other little girls from other countries
Are walking now among crates and bales
While my mother, marooned at the nursing home,
No longer knows the names of her sons.
Where's the soul gone, we wonder among ourselves.
What has it left behind but the few mementos
Shared among us when we closed the apartment?
Dishes and linen boxed for cross-country travel,
Packets of letters she chose to save
For the light they threw on our characters
Or as proof our interests were much like hers.
She must have guessed years back
We'd leave behind the books she treasured—
Accounts of the sufferings of the Jews,
Of Jewish gifts to the planet,
Of the beauties of Jerusalem,
A city she'd have moved to in a minute
After Dad died if one of her three sons
Had been willing to go along.
We wanted the photograph of her nursing class,
St. Louis Jewish Hospital, 1930,
With her at the top, in a circle of her own,
Class president at the graduation.
She'd be glad I found her twenty-part poem
Composed on her sister's twentieth birthday,

A celebration of friendship.
Strange she always remembered her girlhood as an idyll—
Trolley trips with her father to the library,
The sweet smell of her mother's baking—
While her sister still dwells on the shame
Of the shabby cold-water flat they lived in,
How she couldn't bring home a single friend.
Doubtless my mother's habit of affirmation
Rubbed off to some extent on her sons,
Just as it did on the Mexican girl
Who helped for a while with the babies,
Juanita, who wrote me just last year how mother
Was the one teacher who made a difference,
Beginning with the interview. "Juanita," she said,
To the girl sullenly shrugging, "you're too young
To carry a chip around on your shoulder."
Words spoken in a tone that suggested
She'd remembered trying them on herself
And had chosen to give more weight to the moments,
Many or few, when she'd found them helpful.

GLASNOST

I wonder if the changes proclaimed in the headlines
Should push me to get in on the action,
If it's time to question the one-party system
And reduce the checkpoints so a few wishes
Can come and go without inspection,
So visas can be piled at corners for bonfires.
I may be missing a lot when the people
Of Warsaw and Prague gather in public places
To cheer the outcasts of the old regimes as heroes
And elect them ministers while my advisers,
After fifty years of predictable phrases,
Still take it upon themselves to screen every petitioner
And fill the openings on my calendar.
It could be time at least to inspect the line
Of subjects waiting in the anteroom and beyond
Outside in the snow. See how they've grown numb
While I've tinkered with my ten-year plan.
Time to welcome them in and hear their stories,
To send them off rewarded and inspired
To be my ambassadors in the capitals of the world.
No more directives for them to stay in their rooms
With the blinds drawn against thieves and spies.
Let them get out and explore the backlands.
Let them fraternize with the locals.
The new ambassador from Hungary to Nepal
Is a lively example. So what if he earns too little
To hit the bazaars. No outlay's required
To cast a line from a barge in the Irrawaddy.
Plenty of time to share with his fishing companions
The details of his favorite hobby, snorkeling.
He's heard that it's best off Australia

By the Barrier Reef. The fish and coral,
Invisible from the surface, can't be imagined.
There's nothing like it in Europe,
But why should that worry him anymore
If ships to the South Pacific are ready whenever he is
Now the war is over.

HORACE AND I

If it's true I have no church or gospel,
I wonder why I hear what Dante heard
In the genial voice of Horace,
A gloomy undertone.

I don't imagine Horace as Dante does,
A prisoner in an underworld, his lamplit city
Besieged by darkness, shut off from the sun.
And still I'm not convinced of his joy
When he thanks the goddess Fortuna
For his friends and farm, for the lucky gift of a mind
Not insensitive to Greek poetry.

I wonder what better gifts I'm waiting for, what Eden,
If I don't believe the stars shining on the Empire,
Oblivious to any plans but their own,
Shine here as numberless patient worlds.
What will happen that hasn't happened already?
Where am I going that I haven't been?
What pilgrims will I be joining?

This summer I didn't find time
To make my trip, long promised, to the Grand Canyon,
But still I believe next summer will be different
And I'll ride a burro down
And camp with blankets on the stone floor
And sing myself to sleep under the stars.

For now I drive Sundays in farmland,
Wondering what I'd say
If I pulled off at a side road to rest

And spotted Horace waving in welcome,
Calling me to his table under the vines.
"Enjoy this moment before it goes,
This moment no different from the others."
That's what he says as he pulls a chair out
And pours the wine.

Then it's up to me to explain
The gospel of time, how to the faithful
The years are waiting up ahead
To link us with supper music we can't imagine,
How by now the musicians, ghostly as they are,
Are warming up.

DELAWARE PARK, 1990

These five students from China,
Cooking their dinner on the grill by the swings,
May be trying to resist the great temptation
Of feeling orphaned, reminding themselves instead
How they were lonely often back home too
And were happy to be neglected by the authorities.

This country, they could be saying,
May have felt just as alien
To the settlers who arrived early from Europe,
The odd ones who sold their old-country farms
For a passage to a land that for all they knew
Was merely hearsay. As for the Indians,
Who knows what homeland meant to them
When they woke to a vista of hills
Unmarked by clearings, barns, and orchards?

This park could be the one
Their children will play in
As if the benches were made for them,
As if they owned the sun and the clouds,
As if a rain like the one beginning to fall now
Disappointed them only as a friend would,
For reasons they could accept without knowing.

This day, they could be saying
As they gather their blankets, doesn't prove
The life here cold and unwelcoming.
The man who's watched them an hour from his bench
One day won't be a mystery.
They'll be able to guess what he's thinking

Just as they might guess a stranger's thoughts in China.
Today he seems knowing, confident, and remote.
One day he may seem confused and frail,
In need of sponsors. And they'll step forward
With solace they can't offer now.

SPRING LETTER

With the warmer days the shops on Elmwood
Stay open later, still busy long after sundown.
It looks like the neighborhood's coming back.
Gone are the boarded storefronts that you interpreted,
When you lived here, as an emblem of your private recession,
Your ship of state becalmed in the doldrums,
Your guiding stars obscured by fog. Now the cut-rate drugstore
Where you stocked your arsenal against migraine
Is an Asian emporium. Aisles of onyx, silk, and brass,
Of reed baskets so carefully woven and so inexpensive
Every house could have one, one work of art,
Though doubtless you'd refuse, brooding instead
On the weavers, their low wages and long hours,
The fruit of their labor stolen by middlemen.
Tomorrow I too may worry like that, but for now
I'm focusing on a mood of calm, a spirit of acceptance,
Loyal to my plan to keep my moods distinct
And do each justice, one by one.
The people in line for ice cream at the Sweet Tooth
Could be my aunts and uncles, nieces and nephews.
What ritual is more ancient or more peaceable?
Here are the old ones rewarding themselves
For making it to old age. Here are the children
Stunned into silence by the ten-foot list of flavors
From Mud Pie to Milky Way, a cosmic plenty.
And those neither young nor old, should they be loyal
To their favorite flavor or risk a new one?
It's a balmy night in western New York, in May,
Under the lights of Elmwood, which are too bright
For the stars to be visible as they pour down on my head
Their endless starry virtues. Nothing confines me.

Why you felt our town closing in, why here
You could never become whoever you wished to be,
Isn't easy to understand, but I'm trying.
Tomorrow I may ask myself again if my staying
Is a sign of greater enlightenment or smaller ambition.
But this evening, pausing by the window of Elmwood Liquors,
I want to applaud the prize-winning upstate Vouvray,
The equal of its kind in Europe, the sign says.
No time for a glass on your search
As you steer under stars too far to be friendly
Toward the island where True Beauty, the Princess,
Languishes as a prisoner. I can see you at the tiller
Squinting through spume, hoping your charts are accurate,
Hoping she can guess you're on your way.

SHELTER

If, after death, we're free, as the books say,
From the tug of flesh and the tug of spirit,
We should be able to speak with one voice,
To give a lucid answer when we're asked
How we like the room prepared for us
Upstairs in the houses of our friends,
How we like the bedstead and writing table,
The window with the rustling yellow curtains
Overlooking the playground and cornfield.
"This suits us well, this tasteful plainness,"
We'll say, if we can speak,
If our friends, climbing the stairs for talk
Just when we understand what our lives mean,
Don't have to answer for us
And fill our mouths with our old uncertainties
And leave our rooms no wiser than before.
How hard then, left alone, to concentrate
On the books we promised ourselves to study
When we had more time.
Propped by the window,
Watching the children on the swings,
Watching the farmer plowing his field,
We'll have to pray for the patience
That the dead who live now in us
Must often pray for
On the long stretches we're out
Looking for work or happiness
Or the secret of immortal life.
Their room is growing dark and we're still not home.
We're fighting traffic somewhere.
We're drifting to the music on the radio.

And then we're reminded of a song they enjoyed
That we never liked,
And new arguments occur to us
To bolster our side,
New arguments to bolster theirs.

INVITATION

This is your invitation to the Ninth-Grade Play
At Jackson Park Middle School
8:00 P.M., November 17, 1947.
Macbeth, authored by Shakespeare
And directed by Mr. Grossman and Mrs. Silvio
With scenery from Miss Ferguson's art class.

A lot of effort has gone into it.
Dozens of students have chosen to stay after school
Week after week with their teachers
Just to prepare for this one evening,
A gift to lift you a moment beyond the usual.
Even if you've moved away, you'll want to return.
Jackson Park, in case you've forgotten, stands
At the end of Jackson Street at the top of the hill.

Doubtless you recall that *Macbeth* is about ambition.
This is the play for you if you've been tempted
To claw your way to the top. If you haven't been,
It should make you feel grateful.
Just allow time to get lost before arriving.
So many roads are ready to take you forward
Into the empty world to come, misty with promises.
So few will lead you back to what you've missed.

Just get an early start.
Call in sick to the office this once.
Postpone your vacation a day or two.
Prepare to find the road neglected,
The street signs rusted, the school dark,
The doors locked, the windows broken.

This is where the challenge comes in.
Do you suppose our country would have been settled
If the pioneers had worried about being lonely?

Somewhere the students are speaking the lines
You can't remember. Somewhere, days before that,
This invitation went out, this one you're reading
On your knees in the attic, the contents of a trunk
Piled beside you. Forget about your passport.
You don't need to go to Paris just yet.
Europe will seem even more beautiful
After you complete the journey you begin today.

NO SHAME

No shame if you choose in the end
To be buried like an ancient Roman,
At the roadside,
The stone above you crowded with inscription,
Calling the passersby to pause
And read how you served the state,
How the scales of your butcher shop always read true,
How you cared for your small plot, a pious farmer.

No shame to hope for some visitors
Though maybe in life you grew accustomed to solitude,
Content to defend the right
As you spoke in the courtroom
Over the heads of the crowd
To the gods you imagined, who loved perfection.

Having proved you could live alone,
You can reach out in death to others
As the Romans did, with a few true phrases,
Learned early or late.
You who pass by, don't rely on doctors.
They're the ones who brought me here.
Reader of stones, if you're rich
Don't live meanly, as I did,
And stint on feast days.
Traveler, if you're poor, master one skill
So in one thing you can feel superior
And accept without shame,
When the time comes, the help of others.

.

Lying under your stone,
A coin of the realm over each eye,
The fee for Charon's ferry still unspent,
You'll pause in the endless review of memory
And the endless dream of returning
With a disposition that's more agreeable
And listen to the traffic of carts and chariots,
Mule shoes and horseshoes, sandals and clogs.

The few who pause above you
Will be just the ones most open to suggestions.
Their prayers haven't been answered.
Their best schemes have failed them.
Now they bend to read your conclusions.
No shame to teach in a roadside school
Students willing to learn from anyone.

ACKNOWLEDGMENTS

Thanks are due to the editors of the following magazines in which some of the poems first appeared:

The Agni Review ("Infidel"); *American Poetry Review* ("The Messiah" and "Unfinished Symphony"); *Denver Quarterly* ("Adventure," "The Bill of Rights," and "Haven"); *Georgia Review* ("Thanksgiving" and "We and They"); *Kenyon Review* ("Tuesday at First Presbyterian" as "First Presbyterian"); *The New Republic* ("Oedipus the King," copyright 1990 by *The New Republic*); *Poetry* ("Defining Time," "Horace and I," "No Shame," "Spring Letter," and "The Window" copyright 1987, 1988, 1990, 1991 by the Modern Poetry Association); *Prairie Schooner* ("More Snow," "Night Walk," and "The Photograph"); *Salmagundi* ("The Anthropic Cosmological Principle"); *Seneca Review* ("Shelter"); *Shenandoah* ("Local Government" and "The Window in Spring"); *Virginia Quarterly Review* ("My Guardians").

Thanks are also due to the National Endowment of the Arts for a grant that provided the leisure during which some of these poems were written.

Finally, the author wishes to thank the friends who offered indispensable criticism of this manuscript: Charles Altieri, Thomas Centolella, Alan Feldman, Martin Pops, Donald Revell, and Burton Weber.

COLOPHON

The text of this book was set in the typeface Garamond Number 3 and the display type was set in Willow by PennSet, Inc., Bloomsburg, PA.

DESIGNED BY LUCY ALBANESE